Simply
THE BEATITUDES

Other Titles by
Brother Victor-Antoine
d'Avila-Latourrette

Sacred Feasts:
From a Monastery Kitchen

The Gift of Simplicity:
Heart, Mind, Body, Soul

Twelve Months of Monastery Soups:
International Favorites

From a Monastery Kitchen:
The Classic Natural Foods Cookbook

Blessings of the Daily:
A Monastic Book of Days

Blessings of the Table:
Mealtime Prayers Throughout the Year

Simply Living

THE BEATITUDES

Brother Victor-Antoine d'Avila-Latourrette

Liguori

LIGUORI, MISSOURI

Imprimi Potest:
Thomas D. Picton, C.Ss.R.
Provincial, Denver Province
The Redemptorists

Published by Liguori Publications
Liguori, Missouri
To order, call 800-325-9521
www.liguori.org

Library of Congress Cataloging-in-Publication Data
D'Avila-Latourrette, Victor-Antoine.
    Simply living the Beatitudes / Victor-Antoine d'Avila-
Latourrette. — 1st ed.
        p. cm.
    ISBN 978-0-7648-2725-9
    1. Beatitudes. 2. Christian life—Catholic authors. I. Title.
    BT382.D28 2010
    241.5'3—dc22

                                                        2010009348

Liguori Publications, a nonprofit corporation, is an apostolate of
the Redemptorists. To learn more about the Redemptorists, visit
Redemptorists.com.

Printed in the United States of America
14 13 12 11 10   5 4 3 2 1
First edition

*In loving memory of Dorothy Day,
grateful for her friendship in all times and seasons
and for her faithful example of true Gospel living.
She made the living out of the Beatitudes
the centrality of her Christian life
and remains thus an inspiration to many.*

Contents

Simplicity and
the Beatitudes

A Path to Gospel Holiness

"Blessed are the poor in spirit,
     for theirs is the kingdom of heaven.

"Blessed are those who mourn,
     for they will be comforted.

"Blessed are the meek,
     for they will inherit the earth.

"Blessed are those who hunger and thirst
     for righteousness,
             for they will be filled.

"Blessed are the merciful,
     for they will receive mercy.

"Blessed are the pure in heart,
     for they will see God.

"Blessed are the peacemakers,
for they will be called
children of God.

"Blessed are those who are persecuted
for righteousness' sake,
for theirs is the kingdom of heaven.

"Blessed are you when people revile you and persecute you and utter all kinds of evil against you falsely on my account. Rejoice and be glad, for your reward is great in heaven, for in the same way they persecuted the prophets who were before you."

MATTHEW 5:3–12

How are we to understand the Beatitudes? Clearly Jesus was making use of the common Jewish teaching technique of hyperbole to accent God's identification with the weak and the destitute. There is a special divine caring for those who cannot care for themselves. In these beatitudes, Jesus is expressing his burden for the bruised and broken and he invites us to share that burden.

RICHARD J. FOSTER,
FREEDOM OF SIMPLICITY

The Gospels, as they depict for us the life and teachings of Jesus and spell out divine wisdom expressed in human words, are truly the Good News to each of us and to the entire world. The Gospels offer all of us possibilities for a new life that contrasts immensely with our old one of sin and death, a new life that directs our steps into the path of holiness and union with God.

God, in his infinite love, created us for this new life in Christ. He so loved the world, says Saint Paul, that he sent Jesus, his beloved Son, to reconcile us and bring us back to him. Jesus is God's own supreme gift to us, the gift from a Father offering all his children endless possibilities for one day reaching eternal life and happiness with him.

Ever since these Beatitudes were first proclaimed by the Master, they have been a life-giving challenge to all who have tried to follow in the Lord's footsteps.

Through his only-begotten Son, our savior Jesus Christ, we all gain access to the Father and share in the mystery of his divine and eternal life. The Apostle John writes: "God gave us eternal life, and this life is in his Son. Whoever has the Son has life; whoever does not have the Son of God does not have life. I write these things to you who believe in the name of the Son of God, so that you may know that you have eternal life" (1 John 5:11–13).

Among the many lessons full of divine simplicity that Jesus left as testament to us, his followers, are his teachings on what have been called, throughout the centuries, the Beatitudes. We must admit that ever since these Beatitudes were first proclaimed by the Master, they have been a life-giving challenge to all who have tried to follow in the Lord's footsteps. They have been a challenge not only to the people of Jesus' time, who first heard him utter them directly, but also to subsequent generations of believers who sincerely tried to live by them. Throughout the centuries, each generation of Christians have tried to decipher the true meaning of these counsels and their full implications in their personal lives. As the disciples who first heard them pronounced by their Lord and Teacher, we too must ask ourselves: What did the Lord mean by them? What was he really saying? What was he really trying to teach us? And, more importantly, how are we to live by them and put them into practice? These questions continue to surge in our minds and hearts every time we hear this Gospel proclaimed in either Matthew 5:3–12 or Luke 6:20–23. One thing we know for sure is that it is possible to live by them and put them into practice. God never asks the impossible from any of us. Furthermore, the living examples of Our Lady and the Apostles, of the Fathers, and of the early monks and nuns give ample testimony to the real possibility of putting into practice the Beatitudes. We do need, of course, God's grace, a deep spirit of simplicity and prayer, and just plain human willingness to abide by them.

Throughout the centuries, these Beatitudes have revealed themselves to us with their particular colors and nuances, like fresh pages just written, read, or discovered in the Gospels, with their own practical implications for our times, for our lives, right in the here and now. There is such freshness in their utterance, such depth, such authentic Gospel simplicity in the structure of each sentence that they almost sound as if they are being taught and proclaimed by the Lord himself at the very moment we hear them. I always find it deeply meaningful each time I hear them sung in the Eastern Divine Liturgy, or when they are sung as part of the grace before the daily meal in some monasteries in France, or on the Feast of All Saints when they are proclaimed in the Gospel of the day.

It is appropriate indeed to hear the Gospel of the Beatitudes on All Saints Day. For what better path to holiness do we have than truly putting into practice the teachings contained in the Beatitudes? It is not surprising to discover that Jesus used the term "blessed" to initiate each Beatitude sentence. For blessed conveys accurately the meaning and sense he attached to each of them. It is by humbly and simply putting into practice each Beatitude that the kingdom of heaven, the eternal state of blessedness, is promised to us. God, in his mystery, abides in a permanent state of blessedness; and it is to that eternal blessedness, as in a banquet, that we are all invited. To embrace in all simplicity a life based on the teaching and practice of the Beatitudes is to share intimately in the eternal blessedness of God, the very blessed communion state that Jesus shares with his Father and the Holy Spirit.

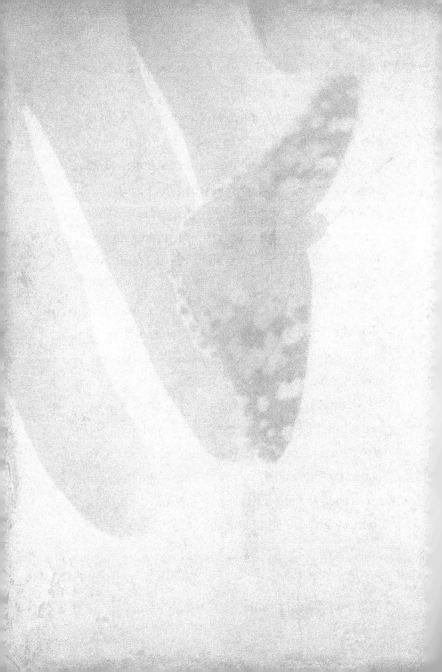

"Blessed are
the poor in spirit,
for theirs is the
kingdom of heaven."

MATTHEW 5:3

*S*ometimes the word "poor" is understood by biblical exegetes as those who are materially poor. There is no doubt in my mind that they are certainly included and particularly addressed in the sentence, as Jesus always showed a particular preference for the materially poor. But since we know the salvation message from the Gospels is for all creatures, poor and rich alike, we know that this Beatitude invitation is addressed to everyone of good will who hears it and who wishes to follow the Lord with true simplicity.

We are all "poor in spirit" as we stand before God our Father naked, empty-handed, in dire need of his love and mercy. God, the all-compassionate

One, always rich in mercy, is there waiting to offer each of us—poor and destitute that we are—the immense gift of his eternal compassion and mercy. How blessed indeed are we to be poor in spirit: poor and in such utter need of God that we are offered as recompense, as gift and reward, the privilege of partaking of God's very own life in his kingdom!

In our contemporary world, poverty in any form would be despised and considered a curse. And yet, Gospel simplicity allows us to look at poverty from another angle, one not always amenable in the eyes of the world: not as an affliction, but as a gift from God. The Scriptures tell us that when Christ entered into this world, he emptied himself, became poor, and took the form of a servant. If God himself embraces a state of poverty, who are we to condemn it?

There are so many lessons that we as Christians

> Gospel simplicity allows us to look at poverty from another angle, one not always amenable in the eyes of the world: not as an affliction, but as a gift from God.

can learn from the mystery of poverty. Yes, it is true we live in a complex world today as the Lord did in his time. There are as many varieties of socioeconomic backgrounds as one can imagine: wealthy people and poor people and everyone in between. And yet the Word of God addresses itself to all people, regardless of their material conditions. The Good News of God's salvation in Christ is offered to all disposed to follow him. And so the wealthy and the materially poor and all those in between are invited to live out the truth contained in this Beatitude. The wealthy are invited to become poor in spirit by becoming detached from their wealth and by sharing it with those in need. If they do so, then blessed are they! And the poor become blessed by accepting their total dependence on a loving Father, who provides for their needs and watches over them. And we all shall share in this state of blessedness, regardless of any economic conditions, when we agree to become poor in spirit in order to follow our Master and Savior, who once was poor and crucified.

Discerning the Gospel
Teaching on Poverty of Spirit

Poverty was not found in heaven. It abounded on earth, but human beings did not know its value. The Son of God treasured it, and came down from heaven to choose it for himself, and so make it precious to us.

ST. BERNARD OF CLAIRVAUX

Christ hungers now, my brethren; it is he who deigns to hunger and thirst in the persons of the poor. And what he will return in heaven tomorrow is what he receives here on earth today.

ST. CAESARIUS OF ARLES

Whenever we meditate on a particular passage of the Beatitudes, we must remember that Jesus taught from the wellspring of his own life. Contrary to many preachers who say one thing and do another, the Lord experienced each of his teachings before entreating others to do the same. Jesus taught the truth as he lived it daily. He knew what it meant to be poor in spirit. As Saint Bernard reminds us in the text quoted above, Christ humbly embraced poverty at the moment of his Incarnation, even though poverty does not exist in heaven. The Incarnation itself is the mystery of God taking and embracing the lowly, poor condition of our humanity. What greater proof is there that the Lord treasured this humble state of poverty than that from the beginning of his life on earth, he chose it for himself? In doing this, Saint Bernard adds, the Lord elevates the often belittled state of poverty to a noble and precious one. More importantly, he elevates the state of all those who

> Jesus taught the truth as he lived it daily. He knew what it meant to be poor in spirit.

are poor. Indeed, it is to those who are poor—those who understand their utter dependence on God—that he promises a sharing in the kingdom of heaven. To those who follow him by seeking to become the poor in spirit, Jesus offers a kingdom so consoling and magnificent that one would trade any wealth and worldly satisfaction for the sake of entering into it.

From the Scriptures, especially the Gospel of Luke, we clearly hear the message of the Lord: preferential treatment for the materially and psychologically poor. It is to the outcast, the dispossessed, the hungry, and the abandoned that Jesus addresses his message of hope and promise at the beginning of his ministry. These people in need are the ones first invited to the blessings of his kingdom. This is not surprising, since it is so often the economically poor and destitute who feel most deeply their utter dependence on God's help. Already in the Old Testament, particularly in the prophet Isaiah, we hear the proclamation that God's long-promised Messiah shall come to bring freedom and salvation to the poor, the outcasts, the lowly, and the rejected ones of this world.

When we consider this particularly Beatitude, we must first acknowledge the materially poor. However, we must also remember that there are others who may not be economically deprived but are poor in other ways. These people too are in deep need of God's mercy and the blessings of his kingdom. Jesus's invitation to become poor in spirit is not only addressed to the materially poor, but to all of God's children—poor, rich, or in-between. We all partake of the poverty and imperfection of the human condition, and thus hunger for the salvation promised by God. Accepting to become poor in spirit means accepting in all simplicity our total dependence on God, as well as giving all the fraternal help we can offer to our brothers and sisters in need.

The Gospel message binds our personal need for God with an honest concern for the poor, the oppressed, and the deprived. It is impossible to achieve true spiritual union with God without being compelled to help improve the welfare of our neighbor: the poor and lonely, our impoverished brothers and sisters. For Jesus, the love of God and the love of a neighbor are two concrete sides of the same coin. The path that leads us to ultimate union with God is the path that leads to compassion, aid, and genuine concern for those who are deprived of even the very essentials of life.

Siblings in true Gospel simplicity, the letter and spirit of this particular Beatitude, means growing daily into a totally non-possessive attitude, relying less on the false security offered by material wealth and becoming ever more dependent on God's gifts and blessings. God alone

We must also remember that there are others who may not be economically deprived but are poor in other ways. These people too are in deep need of God's mercy and the blessings of his kingdom.

is the giver of all good gifts. Only he can provide for our greatest needs as human beings and ultimately satiate the inner longings of our hearts. Accepting the Lord's invitation to become poor in spirit shall free us from the anxiety and transience of wealth. We too will bid goodbye to the burden of useless possessions. Our hearts shall feel liberated from the tyranny of greed and selfishness and instead will open wide to receive the wealth of God's grace and blessings.

Prayer

Come, Spirit of true light.
Come, life eternal.
Come, hidden mystery of God.
Come, nameless treasure.
Come, one who is beyond words.
Come, source of all courage.
Come, true hope of all the saved.
Come, eternal joy.
Come, my life and breath.
Come, consolation of my soul.
Come, O Spirit of truth and grant that
we may be nourished abundantly
by the gift of your presence. Amen.

"Blessed are those
who mourn,
for they will
be comforted."

MATTHEW 5:4

*I*t is hard for Christians and non-Christians alike to understand and accept the message contained in this particular Beatitude. Sorrow, suffering, anguish, grief, and mourning are concepts that carry such negative connotations. Are the realities contained in these concepts what Jesus really addresses as a blessing? Jesus was certainly what is described today as "countercultural," but has he gone too far on this? Are we understanding correctly his endorsement of suffering?

Again, making recourse to the wisdom of Gospel simplicity, we can slowly begin to untangle the meaning of this Beatitude. From the Gospels, we learn that Jesus led a normal human life, that he enjoyed what life had to offer during his time on earth. He did not embrace or seek suffering for its own sake, and when he had to confront it vividly at Mount Olives, just before his Passion, he asked the Father to remove the cup of suffering from him if at all possible. And though the Lord did not go about directly looking for suffering, he knew that we all live in a faulty and corrupted world that carries the burden of sin and the consequence of suffering as penalty. He also knew that it is almost impossible to avoid pain as part and parcel of the human condition. As a matter of fact, he came into the world, paradoxically, to free the rest of us from the burdens of sin by his direct embrace of human suffering on the cross. The transformation of suffering into a state of blessedness, the embracing of it, is one of the deepest mysteries of our Christian faith. We can only accept it, as he did, with grace given from above.

> The transformation of suffering into a state of blessedness, the embracing of it, is one of the deepest mysteries of our Christian faith.

To live the teaching contained in this Beatitude and to put it into practice entails a great deal of prayer and patience on our part. We need patience with ourselves, patience with others, and most especially patience with God as he is patient with us. We are called, as Christians, to accept and recognize the reality of sorrow and suffering in our own lives and in the lives of others. How difficult this is! Oh, and how much faith and help from above we need while undergoing the process! The spirit of this Beatitude challenges us to deal with the ostensibly useless mystery of pain and sorrow in a positive way by considering it a blessing. We can truly ascertain from this how radical indeed the message of the Gospels is. All we can ultimately do in the effort to accept, live, and partake in the mystery of this particular Beatitude is to look at Jesus during those crucial moments of his agony in

> The spirit of this Beatitude challenges us to deal with the ostensibly useless mystery of pain and sorrow in a positive way by considering it a blessing.

the garden of Gethsemane. From him, our Master, we can also learn to turn to the Father in complete trust and abandonment during the hour of trial. It is in the acceptance of God's will, while enduring with Christ our own time of sorrow and distress, that we receive the gift of God's consolation and the needed strength to carry Christ's cross with him. Blessed indeed are those who mourn, for God's consolation shall rest upon them!

Prayer

Lord Jesus Christ, on the evening of your Resurrection, with eyes of faith, your disciples recognized your presence during the breaking of bread. Increase the gift of faith in all of us. May it daily transform our lives, and allow us to discover you anew in our brothers and sisters in need. Keep us always safe under the protection of your love. Amen.

A Gospel Paradox and Mystery: The Cross

Sorrow is one of the things that are lent, not given. A thing that is lent may be taken away; a thing that is given is not taken away. Joy is given; sorrow is lent.

AMY CARMICHAEL, IRISH-BORN MISSIONARY

In sorrow and suffering, go straight to God with confidence, and you will be strengthened, enlightened and instructed.

ST. JOHN OF THE CROSS

By taking up the cross, I received strength against many things which I had thought impossible to deny; but many tears did I shed, and bitterness of soul did I experience, before I came tither.

MARY PENINGTON, ENGLISH QUAKER

To accept the Gospels and to decide to be a disciple of Christ is a counter-cultural act. All of Christ's teachings and the very example of his earthly existence are counter-cultural. The beatitudes, those very straightforward teachings the Lord instilled in the hearts and minds of his followers, are among the most counter-cultural teachings of any master. And the cross itself, the very instrument used by God to accomplish our redemption, is itself a sign of contradiction and one of the most controversial and counter-cultural symbols of all time.

When Jesus accepted to endure the pain and sorrow of carrying and ultimately dying on the cross, he ushered in a whole new paradigm for those who believed in him and would follow him to the end. Through the cross, and that utterly raw form of suffering he endured during his crucifixion, Christ somehow overcame the power of evil. Through his patient endurance of pain, sorrow,

> Through the cross Christ somehow overcame the power of evil.

and seemingly human defeat, Jesus triumphs over the dark powers of the world and opens heaven for us. He pours over us his tender mercy with the graciousness of his immeasurable love.

When Christ invites the disciple to imitate the example of his life, he is inviting him to partake of the mystery and reality of suffering as an integral part of all Christian living. Gently but firmly, the Lord sways the disciple to take up his own cross and follow him. Needless to say, during our earthly journey, we are sometimes confronted with the mystery of suffering, with hardships and sorrow. It is at those very moments when we hear the Lord's voice inviting each of us to identify and share in the mystery of his own suffering. Clearly, according to Gospel teachings, there is an intimate connection between suffering, sorrow, and spiritual growth. But this inner growth comes at a cost—that of

> During our earthly journey, we are sometimes confronted with the mystery of suffering, with hardships and sorrow.

embracing Christ's cross daily and not succumbing to its burden.

Grief, sorrow, suffering—however one may choose to describe it, it is part and parcel of all human existence. Sooner or later it penetrates the life of every one of us. The spirit of this particular Beatitude prepares us to accept the challenge of these harsh realities as they enter into our individual lives. Whatever the cause of our sorrow, this Beatitude gives us the opportunity to bring meaning to an otherwise totally negative experience. Each of us can respond to grief and pain in our own way. Sometimes the pain and sense of loss is such that we feel ready to succumb to its pressure. It is then that we hear Jesus' promise of consolation. His words come to our rescue and fill us with new hope. His promise to relieve us from our pain then becomes deeper than the pain itself. Jesus knew sorrow in his own life and prayed to his Father for deliverance from

> Jesus knew sorrow in his own life and prayed to his Father for deliverance from it.

it. Now, as we traverse our own moment of sorrow, he is there by us to offer the hope and peace of his consolation. As Saint Paul tells us in his letters to the Colossians, "May you be made strong with all the strength that comes from his glorious power, and may you be prepared to endure everything with patience, while joyfully giving thanks to the Father, who has enabled you to share in the inheritance of the saints in the light" (Colossians 1:11–12). For many, suffering is both a harsh daily reality and also a mystery, a mystery that is woven into the very fabric of all human existence. We can try to avoid it, and it would seem logical for us to do so, but sooner or later suffering will meet us again at the crossroads. For those of us who have faith, the only thing to do is to abandon ourselves to God's mysterious plan, trusting in his words that those who suffer shall be consoled. We may not always fathom God's mysterious plan for each one of us, but we can all trust in the Apostle's words: "That all things work unto good for those who love God." As we realistically look for a good end to an experience of grief brought upon us or our loved ones, we can be forever thankful that God is holding us close to him during these trying moments. How much greater our sorrow would be if it were totally devoid of meaning and God wasn't close by to sustain us? Thankfully, as we place our trust in his promise, we begin to experience consolation during our period of grief and find solace under his mighty wings.

Prayer

God of love and tenderness, accept the prayers
and sacrifices we offer you. May our fasting
increase in us a hunger for a deeper sharing
in Christ's death and Resurrection.
Bless us that we may be renewed and
strengthened. Grant this through
Christ, our Lord. Amen.

"Blessed are the meek,
for they will
inherit the earth."

MATTHEW 5:5

*S*implicity has a unique congenial strength that comes from its sense of transparency. Indeed, Gospel simplicity is so transparent that it renders the Lord's teachings luminous, comely, consoling, and always full of divine wisdom for us all. This is particularly true in the teaching concealed behind this Beatitude. When we heed the virtuous quality of meekness, we must remember before anything else pops into our heads the very example of Jesus's life and constant behavior, for he himself was meek and gentle of heart: *Learn from me, for I am meek and gentle-hearted.* Jesus combined in his own personality, his own behavior, both gentleness and the inner strength that springs forth from meekness.

Meekness, as taught in the Gospels, is not a sign of weakness or apathy or passivity as one confronts evil. On the contrary, meekness is a source of inner strength and power. The meek and gentle possess a power which the violent, the angry, the vicious, or the malicious are unable to comprehend or attain. It is a power given from above, an inner power that enables one to resist reacting with violence when confronting aggression and all sorts of evil. A Christian, following in the footsteps of the Master, always pursues nonviolent means for achieving whatever goals he or she embarks upon, making sure that those means never inflict pain or injustice on others.

> The meek and gentle possess a power which the violent, the angry, the vicious, or the malicious are unable to comprehend or attain.

In a contemporary culture such as ours, where violence, greed and hate are perpetuated and greatly glorified, the Christian in contrast quickens the Gospel examples of meekness, gentleness, loving tenderness: all of them God-like qualities. In all simplicity, guided by the Holy Spirit, we slowly begin replacing the abusive and negative values encountered and fostered by present-day culture with the lessons of meekness and gentleness we learn and absorb from the Gospels. This is not a trivial undertaking, and the examples of Saint Benedict, Saint Francis of Assisi, and Saint Francis de Sales, among others, can be a great encouragement to us. They fiercely adhered to these Gospel teachings during their lifetimes and truly put them into practice. They were able to change the minds and behavior of many of those surrounding them.

To those who follow God's ways by practicing the virtues of meekness, gentleness, respect for others, and concern and caring for their neighbor, a promise is made by the Lord. To these disciples, he promises that they shall inherit the earth. The earth is understood here as metaphor and symbol for the kingdom of God. The earth the meek inherit is, after all, the Promised Land itself: the land where all God's creatures live in harmony, peace, and the delight of God's incomparable company.

The earth the meek inherit is the Promised Land itself: the land where all God's creatures live in harmony, peace, and the delight of God's incomparable company.

Jesus entrusts the care of the land to the meek and gentle, for he knows full well they shall treat this great treasure assigned to them with respect and utter reverence. They shall cultivate the earth and make use of its resources as God himself would: wisely, sparingly, and with great simplicity. The earth is not entrusted to us by God to be abused or ill-treated. To the contrary, the earth and its abundance—a symbol of God's own kingdom—is being offered to us as a gift to cherish and protect. By protecting and conserving the land's resources, we shall be able to prove to the Creator that we have indeed become what he wishes us to be: meek and worthy stewards of his creation.

Prayer

Lord God, we bless you for giving us your Word, the Lord Jesus Christ, as a lamp to guide our steps toward you, and as clear light for our path. Bless our neighbors, and give bread, peace, and joy to the world. We ask you this in Jesus' name. Amen.

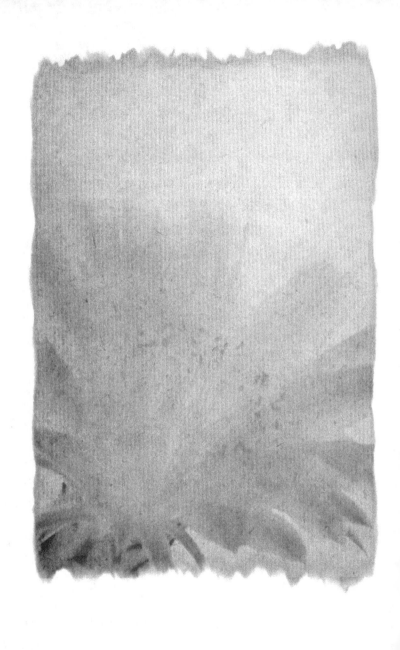

To Be Like Christ:
Meek and Gentle of Heart

Selfish men may possess the earth; it is the meek only who will inherit it from the heavenly Father, free from all defilements and perplexities of unrighteousness.

JOHN WOOLMAN, QUAKER PREACHER

Meekness was the method that Jesus used with the apostles. He put up with their ignorance and roughness and even their infidelity. He treated sinners with a kindness and affection that caused some to be shocked, others to be scandalized, and still others to gain hope in God's mercy. Thus, he bade us to be gentle and humble of heart.

ST. JOHN BOSCO (1815-1888)

We live in times of turbulence, violence, agitation, war, and endless conflict all around us. It is hard to think of the concept and practice of meekness in the midst of such harshness and meanness. We can barely be civilized in our political discourse, never mind try to entertain the notion of gentle meekness as Jesus lived and taught to his disciples.

Meekness and gentleness of heart are not values in our present-day violent culture; however, they are Gospel values required by all who have Christ as their Lord and Master. Our earthly journey toward God demands a gentle docility of heart to the inner prompting of the Holy Spirit and an attitude of meekness and simplicity in all human interaction. As Saint John Bosco taught, it was the practice and method that Jesus used, the example he gave us all, and so it must also be ours.

A humble and meek attitude is not one of weakness. On the contrary, it is an attitude of inner strength.

To work to become "meek and gentle of heart" as the Lord wishes is not always easy. We know for a fact that the ways of the Gospel are rather difficult to follow. One of the basic requirements of those who truly wish to remain "meek and humble of heart" is to learn to practice patience towards our neighbor. We must become meek and gentle of heart not only towards ourselves, but especially in our relation to all our brothers and sisters in the Lord. Meekness does not exist in isolation. It always exists in interaction and relation to others. A humble and meek attitude is not one of weakness. On the contrary, it is an attitude of inner strength, for where we meet conflict and affliction, a meek and humble spirit enables us to remain calm, patient, and peaceful. This is the spirit Jesus exemplified throughout his earthly life.

If we are sometimes tempted to become impatient with others and thus lose our inner core of meekness and humility, we must remind ourselves of the Lord's own patience and tolerance with those same people—and with each of us. If the Lord, who is all holy and perfect, can be so meek, patient, and tolerant of our own imperfections and those of others, why can't we at least try to do likewise?

True spiritual meekness and gentleness of heart are not passive attitudes or virtues. Rather, they demand active daily participation and practice. It is not enough to be patient and wish the welfare of our neighbors. We must go a step further and contribute to that welfare, to the improvement of our neighbors' lives, especially the poor and destitute.

Patience and tolerance are the flip-side of the coin of meekness and humility of heart. With the help of God's grace, we grow daily into a deeper attitude of meekness and gentleness in imitation of Jesus, and we become more tolerant and patient with all those around us. This does not mean giving in to laxity or mediocrity. It simply means accepting others as they are and admitting that any form of judgement belongs to God alone. The Lord is delighted with those who are meek and humble of heart. They are very close to his own heart, which is at all times a fountain of sweetness and mercy to saints and sinners and all those who approach him with trust and confidence. Jesus, meek and humble of heart, make our hearts like unto thine!

"Blessed are those who
hunger and thirst
for righteousness,
for they will be filled."

MATTHEW 5:6

Christ, our Master and Savior, with that unsurpassed simplicity, that remarkable directness of his, states in one of the Gospels: "But strive first for the kingdom of God and his righteousness, and all these things will be given to you as well" (Matthew 6:33). Each of the Beatitudes not only conveys the centrality of the Gospel message, the way Christ expects his disciples to live, but goes even further to give us a true self-portrait of the Master himself. Jesus lived, breathed, and exemplified in his own flesh each Beatitude.

In this particular Beatitude, very conscious of the barriers created by human injustice and by cultural, political, and religious systems that oppressed a great chunk of humanity—the poor, the underprivileged, the despised minorities, the helpless, the undocumented immigrant, entrapped slaves and prisoners alike—Jesus reminds his followers that as much as the human body yearns for food and drink, even more so the heart of the Christian must crave for compassion and human justice for his fellow men and women. And he didn't make exceptions for anyone. All of us, as disciples of such a Master, are called to lift the obstruction components, wherever we find them, that bind our brothers and sisters to a life of oppression and bondage. When we look at the so-called "marginals" of our society, we often find among some of them people who are spiritually and psychologically deprived, and others who are living in material poverty and in miserable physical conditions. Jesus wishes to liberate everyone from whatever forms of oppression in which they find themselves. And he wants us to be his partners and emis-

> Jesus wishes to liberate everyone from whatever forms of oppression in which they find themselves.

saries in this noble undertaking. Jesus undertakes through us, his followers, the work of bringing relief to people's pains: to the spiritually depressed and the psychologically lonely, the materially poor and those in virtual slavery, the hungry and the deprived, the homeless and the dispossessed. He promises to all of them at the same time satisfaction and the vindication of justice. Even the materially wealthy are in great need of experiencing a form of liberation from the bondage of their possessions and earthly attachments and thus must humbly look to the Lord for compassion and mercy.

The role of Gospel simplicity is to teach us to live in complete solidarity with the poor and the deprived, with the hungry and the homeless, with those abandoned by society without hope for a better future. Often, the greatest sin against the poor and those who find themselves in state of misery is the indifference of their fellow Christians, of those who are better off and seemingly lack for nothing. It is the task of the Christian to cast aside the barriers that exist between those who are "satiated and satisfied" and those who lack the bare minimum to survive. With true Gospel simplicity, we must follow the example of Jesus, who was filled with emotion and human compassion every time he encountered people in need. He never bypassed any one of them; on the contrary, he stopped everything else he was doing to care for their needs. The lessons of the Gospel, the very examples in Jesus' life, are clear and very much to the point. Now it is our task as disciples to follow the Master and put into practice the teachings contained in each of the Beatitudes.

Prayer

Lord, our God, through the example of your
only Son, our Lord Jesus Christ, you encourage
us to walk the path of justice and peace,
with special concern and love for the poor,
the oppressed, the downtrodden. Teach us to act
to alleviate the suffering of our brothers and
sisters around the world, through the same
Jesus, your Son and our Lord. Amen.

Justice and Peace Shall Embrace

[The Lord] executes justice for the oppressed.

PSALM 146:7

If you love the justice of Jesus Christ more than you fear human judgment, then you will seek to do compassion.

MECHTILDE OF MAGDEBURGH

It is no good talking sentimentally about love towards the new and hungry nations of the earth unless we are prepared to recognize the justice of their demands.

STANLEY BOOTH-CLIBBORN,
ANGLICAN BISHOP

In the Old Testament, we hear the powerful and unmistakable voices of the prophets rising up against the injustice of their times, cutting across worldly positions, occupations, social or economic statutes, races and nationalities, and defending the rights of the poor and the oppressed—the widows, orphans, strangers, and foreigners. They remind the people of their time that all human beings share the same dignity and are worthy of respect, for they are all equal before God and are his children. Later on in the New Testament, we hear Christ's voice calling for justice and unity among all people, as brothers and sisters who share the same divine life received from one and the same Father of all.

Right here in our country people often separate themselves based on race, nationality, politics, social status, or economic background.

Justice is still very elusive these days, as it was during the time of the prophets and earthly days of Christ. Discrimination, division, and prejudice still exist in our society, and right here in our country people often separate themselves based on race, nationality, politics, social status, or economic background. Two thousand years of Christianity seem to have barely impacted the socioeconomic standing of most of the world population. We, the so-called Christians, have not always heeded the Lord's message to work to make justice a reality for our brothers and sisters, often destitute and oppressed.

Saint Mechtilde of Magdeburgh tells us that if we are clothed with the sense of justice that springs from the Gospel of Jesus Christ, we will seek to act with compassion towards those who are helpless: the poor, the captive, the blind, the undocumented immigrant, and all who are oppressed. This compassion towards the needy is rooted not only in the teachings of the Beatitudes, but also in another counsel from the Gospel that shouts at us to carry each other's burdens.

Part and parcel of our personal conversion, and with it the decision to follow the Lord closely, must include the Gospel imperative to work to change the unjust social structures in our world. We must seek more humane laws in our countries, states, and towns, and attempt to foster the well-being of everyone. To hunger and thirst for justice, according to Christ's counsel, means to work for a just and decent standard of living for all. Wherever he is placed by God in the world, the Christian can be a small fertile seed that is planted to encourage decent and just standards of human living: adequate nourishment, medical care, a solid education, and decent working conditions for all.

> To hunger and thirst for justice, according to Christ's counsel, means to work for a just and decent standard of living for all.

The Scriptures are clear that justice means making possible structures that allow all of us to become more fully human, in the image and likeness of God. This is a true challenge for the Christian, but with the help of God's grace—and by following the example of Jesus—it is possible for us to achieve it. Besides, a tenderhearted attitude of compassion for God's oppressed and defenseless children is a much needed manifestation of the Gospel in today's world. The utter materialism and self-centeredness of contemporary society demands such a witness to the Gospel. The Apostle Saint John firmly reminded us that we only abide in God's love, and he in us, when we open our hearts with compassion to the real needs of others (1 John 3:17).

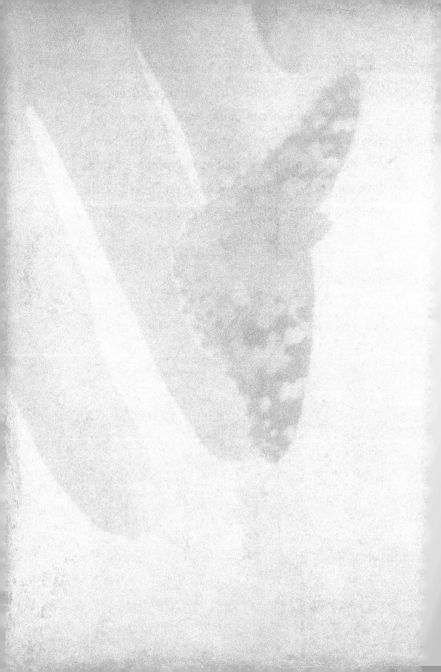

"Blessed are
the merciful,
for they will
receive mercy."

MATTHEW 5:7

*M*ercy is one of the attributes of God. Therefore, it seems obvious that this Beatitude is an open invitation from the Lord to temper our natural thirst for justice with a merciful attitude of heart. We are thus invited to be imitators of God, to be merciful as God is merciful. At times, some of us may find it indeed difficult to put this beatitude into practice, and it may almost seem necessary for us to experience our own need for God's mercy before we start dispensing mercy to others. It is then that a deep attitude of humility and Gospel simplicity come to our rescue. Both humility and simplicity, intertwined as they are by the wisdom of God, inspire us to look deep within ourselves, deep within our own misery and sinfulness, and make us realize that if the Lord shows his mercy and compassion to each of us in spite of our weakness and sinfulness, so must we reciprocate and be imitators of him by showing the same attitude of mercy and compassion towards others. Having ourselves experienced God's tender mercy while still immersed in a state of degradation and utter misery, we are now called to put into practice this particular beatitude by showing mercy and forgiveness with those who injure or offend us. Mercy is very much a divine characteristic, a specific quality by which the Lord wishes to be recognized; thus we are able to call him, "Christ, the Merciful" as he is often addressed in prayer by Eastern Christians. And so it is also with us: when we imitate him and put mercy into practice, we get to be recognized by others as true followers of the Master.

Both humility and simplicity, intertwined as they are by the wisdom of God, inspire us to look deep within ourselves.

The beautiful thing about the Gospel is how easily and with great simplicity it connects all the themes and teachings of Jesus. For instance, the attitude of compassion and forgiveness which we beseech daily in the Our Father is simply the reverse side of the same coin for mercy. When we ask the Lord to forgive our own sins, to show his compassion to us and obliterate our moral debts, we are reminded of another Gospel verse, the one that tells us we must also forgive and be merciful to others as God does it with us: "Blessed are they who show mercy, for they also shall receive mercy" (Matthew 5:7).

In our daily moments of prayer, especially as we recite the Our Father, we must learn to ponder in all simplicity the many times that we ourselves have been the recipients of God's mercy and forgiveness. And as we thank our Father in heaven for his infinite mercies with each of us, we can also ask him for the grace to imitate him closely as we try to dispense mercy and forgiveness to our neighbor. To remain at peace with God means to

In our daily moments of prayer, we must ponder in all simplicity the many times that we ourselves have been the recipients of God's mercy and forgiveness.

be at peace with our neighbor, who is made in God's image as we are. To remain at peace also means we must first forgive and show mercy; we must reconcile even if our neighbor might have hurt us seventy times seven: "Then Peter came up and asked him, 'Lord, when my brother wrongs me, how often must I forgive him? Seven times?' 'No,' Jesus replied, 'not seven times: I say, seventy times seven'" (Matthew 18:21–22).

Prayer

*Lord Jesus Christ, eternal King and Giver
of eternal life, look down with mercy on the
weaknesses of our nature. Illumine us with the
light of your divine knowledge. Shine forth in
our darkened hearts, and make us eager for
your kingdom. Bestow your blessing upon us,
as you blessed many times your friends and
disciples. Bring joy to all those who are merciful
and who share this world with us. Amen.*

To Be Merciful Is to Imitate God

Look, I am going to play the part of God and seat myself on the throne of judgment. What do you want me to do for you then? If you say, "Have mercy on me," God says to you, "If you want me to have mercy on you, do you also have mercy on your brother? If you want me to forgive you, do you also forgive your neighbor?" Can there be injustice in God? Certainly not, but it depends on us whether we wish to be saved.

SAYINGS OF THE DESERT FATHERS

Two works of mercy set a man free: forgive and you will be forgiven, and give and you will receive.

ST. AUGUSTINE OF HIPPO

The simple expression of the publican, "God be merciful to me a sinner," was sufficient to open the floodgates of the Divine Compassion.

ST. JOHN CLIMACUS

Throughout his long discourses with the disciples and his steady preaching to his followers, Jesus unfolded the essence of his message. Some of his followers were immediately ready to accept him, while others contested the veracity of his teachings by asking, "Who do you think you are, anyway?" (John 8:53). One can imagine what the reaction was among many of his listeners when he slowly started communicating each one of his beatitudes. I am sure some of the more hardheaded followers were instantly turned off by several of these hard-to-swallow teachings. Others, perhaps humbler, poorer, more open-minded—and perhaps also more sinful and repentant—were consoled by seeing a ray of hope in the midst of all their woes.

In this particular beatitude, Jesus urges us to be merciful to others as our heavenly Father is merciful with us. Many people find it hard to forgive and thus show mercy to others. Yet the Lord's teaching is clear and concise: we can only reap the benefit of his forgiveness and mercy if we ourselves follow his example and do likewise unto others.

Hearing Jesus proclaim, "Blessed are the merciful, for they will receive mercy," should lift our hearts to a state of new hope. We can be reassured that our lives are in a safe place, surrounded as we are by God's bottomless mercy. Even when we stumble and fall into sin, we know the Lord is ready to welcome us back into his merciful embrace if only we learn to act mercifully toward others.

Indeed, the Christian practice of a merciful heart—of acting mercifully towards others—is one of the high points among all the Gospel teachings. God bestows the floods of compassion towards those who, in turn, are merciful and compassionate toward their neighbors. Having ourselves received the gift of divine mercy, we, the repentant sinners, are now called to go forth and dispense this mercy to all those in need. In doing so, we become witnesses to and dispensers of God's own boundless mercy. Intrinsically and deeply connected to the beatitude teachings in general, and to this one in particular, are the so-called "Works of Mercy," the Lord's pronouncements in Matthew 25:34–40:

"Come, you that are blessed by my Father, inherit the kingdom prepared for you…for I was hungry and you gave me food, I was thirsty and you gave me something to drink, I was a stranger and you welcomed me, I was naked and you gave me clothing, I was sick and you took care of me, I was in prison and you visited me.…Truly I tell you, just as you did it to one of the least of these who are members of my family, you did it to me."

To follow in Jesus' footsteps, to attune our minds and hearts to receive the great gift of his abundant mercy, we must in all Gospel simplicity follow the Master's own example. It is consoling to know that when we feed the hungry and provide drink to the thirsty, clothe the naked and give shelter to strangers, visit the sick and prisoners in jail, we do all this to the Lord himself. In the Gospels there is no room for an arrogant or self-righteous attitude, such as that of the Pharisee. We are all poor sinners in dire

> God bestows the floods of compassion towards those who, in turn, are merciful and compassionate toward their neighbors.

need of God's mercy. The Christian's great challenge, as a member of God's family and a humble follower of Christ, is to incorporate the Lord's own example into our daily lives, and to respond with a kind, compassionate, and merciful heart to the needs, weaknesses, and demands of others. In doing this we find our true joy, for as Saint John Chrysostom writes, "Mercy imitates God and disappoints Satan."

"Blessed are
the pure in heart,
for they will see God."

MATTHEW 5:8

*A*s we meditate on the meaning of this particular beatitude, we must make an effort to go beyond the usual understanding we generally attach to the word "pure." Some translators use the word "clean" instead of "pure," and thus render the text, "Blessed be the clean of heart, for they will see God." In some ways, the word "clean," with its incontestable implication of wholesomeness, simplicity, uncontamination, innocence, and tidiness, comes close to the original understanding granted to this particular beatitude in the early Church. One could also translate the text by saying: "Blessed be those with a heart adroit...." Adroit here suggests "singlemindedness" or an "unpolluted" heart or mind. The early Christians, especially the early desert monks and nuns who applied themselves seriously to the practice of the beatitudes, essentially understood this particular beatitude to mean something that deeply affected their entire lives. For them, this beatitude went directly to the core, essence, and purpose of the Christian life.

In the Scriptures, the word "heart" implies the organ that is the very center and source of life. When the Bible speaks of the heart, it implies the totality of the person. For in the Semitic conception and its languages, the heart always represents the entire person. When Jesus invites his disciples to become pure or clean of heart, he is asking them to become totally, wholly God-centered and to give their undivided attention to God alone. It is by pursuing this path with total simplicity that the Christian arrives to the reward attached by the Lord to this beatitude—the vision of God.

According to the monastic tradition, especially the teachings of Saint John Cassian (so influential on the thoughts of Saint Benedict himself), purity of heart allows the monk (the Christian) to return to the center of his being, where God dwells and where he is most present. Indeed, the Holy Gospels never cease to remind each of us that the kingdom of God is within us—within the depths of our own hearts and not anywhere else. To lose sight of that unique place, the center of our own being, is to diminish our capacity for the genuine purity of heart required for the vision of God. Purity of heart is not achieved in a single day, month, or even a year. It is rather the product of a long, slow process, a process that is at times cumbersome and monotonous in character. By pursuing this tedious, prosaic inner activity of the slow process of conversion and true repentance—with complete simplicity of heart—the ordinary Christian, monastic or not, is led by the Holy Spirit to the ultimate reality of communion with God. This is the goal and promise conferred upon those who take the invitation to follow the ways of this beatitude seriously.

Seeking the Vision of God

If I prayed God that all men should approve of my conduct, I should find myself a penitent at the door of each one, but I rather pray that my heart may be pure towards all.

AMMA SARAH, DESERT MOTHER

The aim of our profession is the kingdom of God or the kingdom of heaven. But our point of reference, our objective, is a clean heart, without which it is impossible for anyone to reach our target.

SAINT JOHN CASSIAN

Be pure, still, learn to yield and climb to darkest heights;

Then you will come o'er all to contemplate your God.

ANGELUS SILESIUS

The beatitudes, the simple and yet challenging way Jesus traces for his followers, could well be called a Gospel "manifesto." Jesus saw in the religious teachers of his times the wearisome burdens they laid upon others with punctilious and trivial practices. He often spoke of them as being deceitful and dishonest with the people. These burdensome practices were more spiritually debilitating to the followers and did not lift them to something better.

In contract to these so-called teachers, Jesus offered his listeners the plain, simple, straightforward teachings of the beatitudes. The practice of the beatitudes, difficult as they may sometimes be, offers to us all a true and honest way of journeying towards God. They sparkle with simplicity, joy, trust, and utter truth. As we make our small daily efforts to live out these teachings, we experience the sort of inner liberation that Jesus promised to those who followed his

> The beatitudes, the simple and yet challenging way Jesus traces for his followers, could well be called a Gospel "manifesto."

way. The beatitudes liberate us from the inside, from negative and useless practices, and direct our glances towards the single purpose of following the way of God.

This particular beatitude counseling us to become pure and clean of heart has as its sole purpose the preparation and orientation of our hearts towards its ultimate end: the eternal vision of God. In the beatitudes, as elsewhere, the Lord uses a certain pedagogy (or teaching method) to enlighten the minds and hearts of his listeners. To those who abide by a certain practice, he promises a corresponding reward. That is, to those who strive to increasingly purify and cleanse their hearts, he promises they shall see God.

Following the ancient Jewish tradition, Jesus attaches a particular meaning to the heart. The heart, according to its biblical understanding, is not only an organ where human feelings reside. It is much more. For the ancient Jews, the heart constituted the very center of the person—the center and source of all life. All a man's attributes converged and had their beginnings and ends in the heart: life, mind, thought, will, emotion, love, hate, repentance. Thus we see that when Jesus demands of us a pure heart as a prerequisite to attaining the vision of God, he is really asking us to cleanse our innermost of all unnecessary clutter and orientate the totality of our being towards the quest of God alone.

Saint Benedict, following the tradition and teachings of Saint John Cassian, makes the quest for God, *quaerendum Deum*, the sole purpose of all monastic life. Both Saint Benedict and Saint John Cassian invite the Christian monk to become God-centered by the practice of a certain simplicity that allows the heart to be totally attentive to God alone. When the heart learns to focus on God and refuses any form of clutter or distraction from that purpose for which it was created, it slowly begins to perceive in its inner horizon a divine presence. As we keep striving daily to

The practice of the beatitudes, difficult as they may sometimes be, offers to us all a true and honest way of journeying towards God.

practice God's word and thus grow closer to this presence, our inner eyes begin to recognize him present in all things—and most especially in the very depths and center of our own being.

Prayer

God, our Father, teach us to live the gospel
with hearts that are pure in a true spirit of joy,
simplicity, mercy, and love for one another.
We ask you this in Jesus' name. Amen.

"Blessed are the
peacemakers,
for they will be called
children of God."

MATTHEW 5:9

ll of the beatitudes have an actuality totally of their own. Each of them carries a timeless element, one always pertinent to the life of the Christian, of the disciple. The Lord's call to become a peacemaker and to renounce violence at all times is not an easy one, but neither is the one commanding us to love our enemies. It is when we are confronted with these hard teachings from the Master that we realize the practice of true Christianity is not a comfortable one; that indeed it is a difficult task we are given when we are proposed heeding the counsels and teachings of such a Master. I think the particular grace of true simplicity in this instance is to portray for us clearly and without compromise the cost of true discipleship.

Throughout the centuries there have always been people trying to interpret how a Christian must respond to the evil of violence, going so far in some cases as to justify the recourse to weapons, thus rendering violence for violence. And yet, what we learn unapologetically from the simplicity of the Master's teachings is that we are given only one alternative, one choice: that of working for and promoting peace between individuals, families, nations, churches, and all other people and groups in all situations. The Christian is invited by this particular beatitude to heed the words and example of the Lord by fostering understanding, healing, and harmony between peoples in all conflicting situations and on every occasion where he encounters alienation and discord. Jesus doesn't simply tell us to keep peace of

> Jesus doesn't simply tell us to keep peace of mind or peace in our hearts: he commands us to actively become peacemakers.

mind or peace in our hearts: he commands us to actively become peacemakers. It is not sufficient to simply just wish or pray for peace. We are all called to undertake the work for peace according to our means and circumstances in life.

The Lord's exhortation to become peacemakers is one that was readily embraced by the early Christians very fervently. There is a long tradition in the Christian church of people who make a commitment to the renunciation of all violence. In the fourth century, when Saint Martin of Tours became a Christian while still a soldier in the Roman Legion, the first thing he did was to lay aside his sword and all his arms. When questioned why he did that, his simple response was, "Now I am a soldier of Christ and the soldier of Christ is not permitted the use of arms." As always, the understanding and response given by a saint is clear, simple, to the point, without the mincing of words. The saints, throughout the ages, knew clearly what the teachings of Jesus were on this matter, and for them there was no compromise. This tradition of pacifism and peacemakers, of actively being involved in the works of peace, has been upheld throughout time by countless monks and nuns, especially the children of Saint Benedict who made PAX their own motto and ideal for their monastic life; by great friars such as Francis of Assisi and his followers; by the so-called peace churches: Quakers, Shakers, and Mennonites, among others; and even in our present day by Catholic Workers and Catholics involved in the international Pax Christi movement.

Simplicity tells us that all real and honest peacemaking begins first in our own hearts. It is impossible to pursue the works of peace while being in conflict with ourselves, with God, or with our neighbor, who is our brother. This is why the Lord commands us that before we approach the table of the Eucharist, we must first reconcile and make peace with our brother or sister—whomever we have conflict with. "So when you are offering your gift at the altar, if you remember that your brother or sister has something against you, leave your gift there before the altar and go; first be reconciled to your brother or sister, and then come and offer your gift" (Matthew 5:23–24). Simplicity tells us that peace is a gift from God, but this means an active gift, one in which we get involved ourselves by actively striving after peace as Saint Benedict reminds us in the Holy Rule.

Gospel simplicity wisely alerts us that to become true peacemakers in our day we must actively cultivate the works of justice. As Pope Paul the VI reminded the world, there cannot be peace in the world without justice. We must acknowledge those structures in our present society that are unjust and corrupt and work for positive change through non-violent means. We can also give concrete witness to the power of this beatitude by our participation in the political process. One concrete mean of fostering peace is to work to elect to positions of responsibility fellow peacemakers, people of conviction who wish to

> Becoming a peace artisan—a peacemaker—implies great courage, fidelity to God's Word, much prayer, and hard work.

change the unjust conditions in our world that lead to conflict and destruction, people who are willing to abide by the teachings of Jesus regarding justice and peace, people who under all circumstances make a complete refusal to war. For the Christian, war is never an option, for he or she comprehends the Gospel teaching that "all who take the sword will perish by the sword" (Matthew 26:52).

Becoming a peace artisan—a peacemaker—implies great courage, fidelity to God's Word, much prayer, and hard work. We must quietly and with Gospel simplicity foster the development of true peace in our world. We must do this in a Christian way, without pride, coercion, manipulation, deception or any other negative means. We must make the radical choice of the Gospel, and of the methods embodied in the Gospels, as our true and only guide, the source of our inspiration, and the one that sets the tone for all our attitudes. Eventually, helped by deep faith and the strength that comes from prayer, we shall discover the power of this same Gospel to make all things right among people, humbly triumphing over the seeds of destruction and evil and making the peace that comes from God a permanent reality in our world.

Prayer

O Eternal God, origin of divinity,
good beyond all that is good, fair beyond all
that is fair, in whom there is calmness, peace,
and harmony: make up for the dissensions
which divide us from each other and bring us
back into the unity of love, that to your divine
nature we may bear some resemblance.
We ask this through the grace, the mercy,
and the tenderness of your only begotten Son,
Jesus the Christ, our Lord. Amen.

BASED ON A PRAYER BY
DIONYSIUS OF ALEXANDRIA

The Peaceful Kingdom

For the kingdom of God is not food and drink but righteousness and peace and joy in the Holy Spirit. The one who thus serves Christ is acceptable to God and has human approval. Let us then pursue what makes for peace and for mutual edification.

ROMANS 14:17–19

In the quotation above, Saint Paul, deeply sensitive to the teachings of the Master, instructs the Romans to work for peace and to become peacemakers themselves. Saint Paul assures his disciples that in abiding by the spirit and letter of this beatitude, pursuing steadily the works of peace, they shall be rewarded with the possession of the kingdom of God, a kingdom of justice, peace, and joy in the Holy Spirit. To become a true peacemaker after the image and example of the Lord himself is to accept the risk of being controversial, counter-cultural, and thus to often get rejected. It takes a great deal of faith in God's words and an inner fortitude to accept the challenge to become a peacemaker in our time. To work for peace is to accept the ministry of reconciliation among all people, among those hostile to each other, among nations at war, among family, neighbors, and churches involved in discord.

> All of the beatitudes are tightly intertwined, and thus are the actions of those who thirst for justice and work for peace for the sake of the Gospel.

The Christian peacemaker needs to imitate the Lord in his interactions with others. Jesus shows in the Gospel a great deal of humility, simplicity, and sincerity, as well as special tact and wisdom as he interacts with others. It is never a question of being pushy or manipulative, of coercing or forcing others to accept his way. On the contrary, to all he gives is this invitation: "Learn from me, for I am meek and humble of heart." The Lord, by his very conduct and example, shows his disciples that true peace is achieved by inner conversion and a change of heart and attitude in each of us. This change of attitude allows us to interact and relate to others as Jesus did in his time: sincerely, peacefully, with simplicity, and in a straightforward manner.

All of the beatitudes are tightly intertwined, and thus are the actions of those who thirst for justice and work for peace for the sake of the Gospel. To truly become a peacemaker, one must also embrace fully the call to work for justice: "Blessed are they who hunger and thirst for righteousness, for they will be filled." The works of justice, the works of mercy, and the works of peace are all necessary to receive and expand the kingdom of God on earth. As true disciples of Jesus, we accept the Gospel challenge to live out these beatitudes openly in our world today, in the midst of society and the Church. Thus we become the Lord's living witnesses, promoting and extending the kingdom of God—a kingdom of justice, peace, and joy in the Holy Spirit. The prophet Isaiah portrays vividly the image of this just and peaceful kingdom in beautiful poetic language. Our work and challenge as Jesus' disciples is to labor for its implementation on earth:

A shoot shall come out from
      the stock of Jesse, and a branch
          shall grow out of his roots.
The spirit of the Lord shall rest on him,
    the spirit of wisdom and
understanding,
      the spirit of counsel and might,
      the spirit of knowledge
         and the fear of the Lord.
His delight shall be in the fear of the Lord.

He shall not judge by what his eyes see,
    or decide by what his ears hear;
but with righteousness
    he shall judge the poor,
    and decide with equity
    for the meek of the earth;
he shall strike the earth with the
    rod of his mouth,
    and with the breath of his lips he shall
    kill the wicked.

Righteousness shall be the belt
 around his waist,
 and faithfulness
the belt around his loins.

The wolf shall live with the lamb,
 the leopard shall lie down with the kid,
the calf and the lion and the fatling together,
 and a little child shall lead them.
The cow and the bear shall graze,
 their young shall lie down together;
 and the lion shall eat straw like the ox.
The nursing child shall play over the hole
of the asp,
 and the weaned child shall put its hand
on the adder's den.
They will not hurt or destroy
 on all my holy mountain;
for the earth will be full of the knowledge
of the Lord
 as the waters cover the sea.

ISAIAH 11:1–9

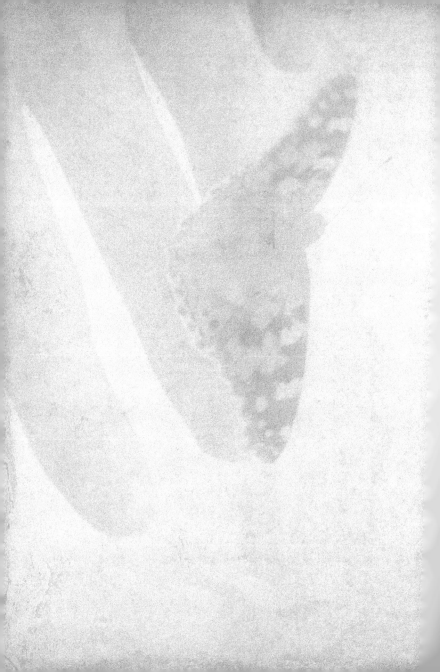

"Blessed are those who are persecuted for righteousness' sake, for theirs is the kingdom of heaven.

"Blessed are you when people revile you and persecute you and utter all kinds of evil against you falsely on my account. Rejoice and be glad, for your reward is great in heaven, for in the same way they persecuted the prophets who were before you."

MATTHEW 5:10–12

As we pray and meditate on the teachings of the beatitudes, one thing that becomes immediately evident to us is the fact that all the beatitudes are closely related. We cannot consider one beatitude isolated from the others. Jesus proclaimed the beatitudes as a way of life for his disciples, for all his followers. And as we heed the call from the Master, we his followers must humbly, simply, and in all earnestness learn to incorporate all of the beatitudes into our own personal lives. This is the great challenge the beatitudes present to each of us.

When we consider this particular beatitude and all its implications, we realize that no sensible person, no one among us in the right mind, makes the choice to be persecuted and to suffer. It is not in our nature to be masochistic or to seek insults and slander. And I don't think this is what Jesus was saying as he uttered this beatitude. What I think he implied on this particular beatitude—and he gave us the example of his own actions as proof—is that there are times when God allows us to undergo the experience of suffering and persecution for the sake of our own good, sometimes for the welfare of others, and, of course, always for the sake of the kingdom of God. There is forever a cost to all true discipleship, and Jesus didn't mince words when he counseled his disciples that in order to follow him they must also take up the cross as he did himself. Jesus, the Son of the living God, was rejected, calumniated, persecuted, forced to carry the cross, and even died crucified on it—all for the sake of reconciling the world, each of us sinners, to the Father. He accepted to

God does not wish to impose suffering on us out of vengeance or chastisement or any other human reason.

be condemned by his fellow men and crucified by the Romans for the sake of our salvation. Through his own personal sufferings, he wished to open the doors to the kingdom for all and for all time.

Sometimes we are asked why bad things happen to good people who faithfully try to follow the Lord. I always respond humbly and with simplicity that this is a great mystery. But it is a mystery that hides behind the unfathomable love of God. For if God the Father, who infinitely and tenderly loved his own Son, allowed him to undergo such human suffering to the very end of his life, there must be a divine motive or reason behind all redemptive suffering. God does not wish to impose suffering on us out of vengeance or chastisement or any other human reason. The only reason he allows it or permits it in our lives is because at the end, a greater good comes out of it. Jesus suffered intensely during his Passion, from the agony in the garden to his last breath on the cross, but out of all that came the priceless gift of our redemption, the reconciliation of humanity, and the whole world with God, its author and creator.

Gospel simplicity provides the grace, the strength, and the motivation to endure the mystery of suffering when the Lord permits it in our lives. We shall never know with certainty the real reason for its role in our lives, but one thing we can be sure of is God's infinite love for each of us. The Father, in allowing us to share in the sufferings and persecution Jesus went through for our sake, brings us closer in union and deeper conformity with his only begotten Son, the Son who is the source of his eternal joy. And as true disciples of the Lord, called to endure from time to time the pain and mystery of the cross, we must always keep in mind that at the end, the joy of the resurrection awaits each of us. *Per crucem ad lucem.* May the Lord grant that one day, through the pain of the cross, we will arrive safely to the joy of eternal Light.

> Gospel simplicity provides the grace, the strength, and the motivation to endure the mystery of suffering when the Lord permits it in our lives.

Prayer

Blessed are you, merciful Father. You sent
to the world your beloved Son, the Lamb of
God, to endure the sufferings of the cross and
thus accomplish the redemption of your people.
Grant through his passion and cross that
we be delivered from darkness and all evil.
Give us strength to continue our journey
toward the glory of the resurrection.
We ask this in Jesus' name. Amen.

Living A God-Centered Life

Lord Jesus Christ,
Our Savior and Divine Master,
You are the Holy One of Israel,
the light of the world,
the life that sustains our lives
and the truth that enlightens
our minds and hearts
on our way to the Father.
We seek to follow your example
by striving to live the beatitudes
in true Gospel simplicity.
We know from your teachings
that the practice of the beatitudes,
challenging as they may be,
are part and parcel of true discipleship
and an essential part of being a Christian.

Send your Holy Spirit upon us
to fortify us and to give us the wisdom,
the courage, and the incentive
to choose always the amazing and humble way
of the beatitudes.
In all things,
we wish and pray to be like you,
    our Master and guide,
leading true God-centered lives
by the inspiration of your Holy Spirit
and the daily practice of the beatitudes.
Have mercy upon us, Lord,
and bestow upon us your blessing
that we may always seek to imitate and
accompany you
on our journey home towards God.
Amen.

The Beatitudes in the Present Moment

O that today you would listen to his voice!
Do not harden your hearts,
as at Meribah…

PSALM 95:7-8

The Beatitudes are a call to us to see ourselves,
to live with ourselves, in a way that probably
does not come easily to most of us.

SIMON TUGWELL

*T*he Gospel reading for the Feast of All Saints, appropriately, is the one on the Beatitudes. In choosing this particular Gospel text, the Church is proclaiming to the faithful that the concrete living out of the Beatitudes is a sure path to holiness. The message and practice of the Beatitudes unites all members of God's family—those in heaven and those on earth. The Beatitudes are implicit in the mystery of the communion of saints.

This daily living out of the Beatitudes somehow transforms the ordinary Christian into a saint. Looking at the example of the Master, we see how Jesus clothed each moment of his life with the practice of the Beatitudes. This he did assiduously, concretely, faithfully, day after day.

The practice of the Beatitudes does not exist in the abstract, only in the concrete; as such, each Beatitude is meant to be lived at a precise moment—in the "today of God," not yesterday or tomorrow. The more we try to understand the message of the Sermon on the Mount, the more we realize its practice demands a conscious appreciation of how we can make the Beatitudes real at any moment.

Once we make the serious decision to follow the Lord daily, closely, we must search for ways of incorporating his teachings on the Beatitudes into the very core of our lives. This demands vigilance on our part, a special attention to the unfolding of each moment as it occurs.

> Each Beatitude is meant to be lived at a precise moment—in the "today of God," not yesterday or tomorrow.

When we find it difficult to keep close attention to the moment, we can pray to the Holy Spirit to instigate this inner attitude in us, to awaken us to his promptings, to inspire us to discover the beauty and reality of each Beatitude at the precise moment we need it most. Eventually, as each moment of our day and life unfolds, we will receive the grace to live and act as Christ did during his earthly life—as the saints did themselves while trying to follow in his footsteps.

The burden of our daily duties, as well as the mental and psychological burdens that often spring from our concerns and worries, can sometimes distract us from keeping the memory of God alive in the intimacy of our hearts. Life becomes so complicated at times that seldom do we take time to withdraw to a quiet place, as Jesus often did, to recapture our spiritual equilibrium. Our daily worries have such an impact in our psyches, in our lives, that sometimes as we project a future solution to them, we altogether forget to make the most of the present moment—the here and now—allotted to us by God.

Today, with all of us caught up in our so-called "careers," trying to make a living for ourselves and our families, we are confronted with the problem of "busy-ness," what is often called the "sickness of our times." This relentless busy-ness seems to overcome us all. Our lives often seem to lack direction; we are made to go around and around endlessly, nonstop from morning till night, without a sense of purpose as to where we are heading. As we experience this sense of meaninglessness, we often get depressed and are overwhelmed by a certain fatigue. These are chronic symptoms of a life that has lost its balance, its center, its sense of aim. It is often very difficult to escape a chronic situation such as the one described here. What can we do then? How can we re-invent our lives from another perspective?

For those spiritually inclined and who cultivate seriously the desire for God, there is hope and help on the way. We can start by looking at the life of Jesus in the Gospels and learn from his example. One of the first things we notice is the striking simplicity of his ways, his behavior, and his teachings. He makes radical simplicity a mark of true discipleship. He not only teaches about simplicity, but he encourages his disciples to practice it: "Look at the birds of the air; they neither sow nor reap nor gather into barns, and yet your heavenly Father feeds them. Are you not of more value than they? And can any of you by worrying add a single hour to your span of life?" (Matthew 6:26–27).

In the biblical passage quoted above, we perceive Jesus teaching to his disciples two very concrete lessons in Gospel living: simplicity and attention to the present moment. He tells them that tomorrow will take care of itself. We realize that it is all about today, the today of God, that we must be concerned. This simplicity of mind and heart, of lifestyle, allows us to rediscover the presence of God in the immediacy of the present moment, the very moment in time our lives unfold. Jesus firmly teaches us, and we are also thus reminded by the Desert Fathers and Mothers not to look for God elsewhere or at other times. Instead, we are all invited now, at this very moment, to meet and encounter God today and listen to his voice. Our bodies and minds may find themselves engrossed

> We are all invited now, at this very moment, to meet and encounter God today and listen to his voice.

in multiple tasks, but through inward simplicity, both mind and heart can find their way back to the heart of God. God is the center of our being, and it is toward him alone that we must gravitate at all times, constantly, and in all occasions. Nothing is more important than that.

At times, in the midst of endless occupations, we may try to escape the burden they bring by making other plans and rearranging our future. However, if we try to live in the present moment, we realize the future does not yet exist. Simplicity makes us aware that we only have the present, that this present moment is terribly important and most intensely vital to our spiritual journey. The present moment is the time chosen by God to give himself to us. It is today that we are invited to listen and ascertain his voice. It is now that we must open up our empty hearts in sincere offering to him. It is easy to look back on the past and all its intricacies, as it is easy to make plans for the future and all its uncertainties. However, Gospel simplicity is there to remind us we no longer possess the past, our yesterdays are done and gone and our tomorrows are in the hand of God. Simplicity asserts once and for all times that we only have the present, that we are only alive in the present. We must be careful not to waste the present hours, for they belong to God. Our God is the God of the present, of the here and now, and it is at that precise moment that we are invited to dwell and be united with him.

Prayer

Lord, our God, You invite us daily
to enter into the mystery of your presence.
You transcend time and space
and dwell in the eternal now.
May your peace, which transcends
all understanding,
keep us rooted in the knowledge and
love of your only Son,
Our Lord Jesus Christ.

Acknowledgments

Unless otherwise noted, quotations are from *The Doubleday Christian Quotation Collection*, compiled by Hannah Ward & Jennifer Wild. New York: Doubleday, 1998. Collection copyright © 1997 by Hannah Ward & Jennifer Wild.

Excerpt from *Freedom of Simplicity: Finding Peace in a Complex World* by Richard J. Foster. London: Hodder & Stoughton, 2005. Copyright © 1981 by Richard J. Foster.

The prayers in each section are adapted from *Blessings of the Table: Mealtime Prayers Throughout the Year*, by Brother Victor-Antoine d'Avila-Latourrette. Liguori, MO: Liguori/Triumph, 2003. Copyright © 2003 by Brother Victor-Antoine d'Avila-Latourrette.

Quotation of Mechtilde of Magdeburgh is from *Beguine Spirituality: An Anthology*, ed. Fiona Bowie, transl. by Oliver Davies. London: SPCK Publishing, 1989.

Quotations of Mary Penington and John Woolman are from *Quaker Faith and Practice*, published by Religious Society of Friends (Quakers) in Britain, 1994.

Sayings of the Desert Fathers and of Amma Sarah are from *The Wisdom of the Desert Fathers*, transl. by Benedicta Ward. Oxford: S.L.G. Press, 1975.

Brother Victor-Antoine d'Avila-Latourrette is resident monk at Our Lady of the Resurrection Monastery near Millbrook, New York, a monastery that lives under the rule of Saint Benedict. There he cooks and tends the garden that supplies both the monastery and the local farmers' market.